Globi
at the Airport

Publisher: Globi Publishing
Creator of the character Globi: Robert Lips
Story and illustrations: Heiri Schmid
Story and text: Jürg Lendenmann
English translation: Eric and Margaret Mace-Tessler
English editor: Stephen Snart

Dear Friends of Globi,

Since you are holding this book in your hand, I presume that you – like Globi – are fascinated by flying. It is easy to understand because I am too. Few places are as multi-faceted, exciting and lively as an airport. Once you have been inside one, you will look forward to visiting many more.

Zurich Airport is Switzerland's gateway to the world and an important transportation hub. From here you can fly to over 170 cities in more than 60 countries. In 2008 more than 22 million people departed, arrived, or caught a connecting flight from here. Every day over 750 airplanes land or take off. The movement of airplanes before take-off and after landing is overseen by the control tower. There are three runways and three docks in Zurich Airport. The runways are checked four times a day, because security is the highest priority in Zurich Airport.

Zurich Airport is situated to the north of the city of Zurich and is itself very much like a city. Approximately 24,000 people work there for some 270 companies. There is a train station, a bus station, multi-level car parks, buildings, restaurants, shopping centre, hotel and parks. A fire brigade, a rescue service and the air rescue service (REGA) are also stationed in the area surrounding the airport. A large conservation area, located partly within and partly outside the airport site, provides a habitat for many species of plants and animals. Did you know, for example, that foxes, rabbits and owls live in the airport?

With over 300,000 visitors annually, Zurich Airport is also one of the most popular tourist destinations in Switzerland. From the observation towers you gain a fascinating insight into air traffic events. A guided bus tour takes you past the hangars, the work-shop, the rescue vehicles and then over the airport ramp up to the runway intersection. From there you have a first-rate view and can observe the airplanes taking off from less than one hundred meters away. Without question you are closer to flight activities in Zurich Airport than any other airport in the world. You can even celebrate your birthday here – with a supervised children's party that includes fun activities and dessert as well as a guided Airport Experience Tour.

Whatever your reason for coming to Zurich Airport, I wish you much happiness and pleasure during your visit.

Zurich Airport

Thomas E. Kern, Director

To Zurich on this very day
brought from his birthplace far away
comes a monkey to the airport,
and Globi's there to lend support.

But the customs forms he will need
are missing – all of them, indeed.
Though it may seem unfair and mean,
he must be put in quarantine!

Globi will care for his every need
for a good two weeks, as agreed.
Yet the airport is the kind of space
where many happenings take place.

Exciting adventures to admire
involving snakes and thieves and fire
await our hero in profusion,
right to the story's conclusion.

No more should be given away.
Read what Globi does each day
and you will see that it's quite true,
the airport will fascinate you.

We need to make just one point more,
for you'll be wondering, we're sure,
if Globi acts in the right way.
Not always, we're sorry to say.

"Hello, Globi, my name is Hector."
"Hello, Mr. Zoo Director!"
"Our little monkey comes today.
Can you please meet him right away?"

From deep in Brazil came the flight,
that bore the creature through the night.
The young traveller, small and meek,
in the North will be unique.

The landing, as well as the flight,
he's withstood – it took all his might.
At once, he is taken away
to Birdsong Street without delay.

Because he is so very shy,
he will not eat nor even try.
Fruit and lettuce he will not touch,
forcing him won't do very much.

Globi grabs a broom and, you see,
he looks just like the little monkey.
The creature's fears begin to fade,
thanks to the trick that Globi played.

Convinced Globi is one of his kind,
he hugs him with an easy mind.
"Leo is what I will call this fellow,"
Globi thinks and both feel mellow.

The Lion Monkey Arrives

Dr. Hotz upsets Globi's plans today.
"In quarantine Leo must stay.
He must remain because, I fear,
his customs papers are not here."

Yes, in his cage Leo must stay.
For him there is no other way.
This place is empty and quite bare,
not a single plant grows in there.

So at once Globi goes away
to buy Leo greenery that day.
To the cage he brings all kinds
of jungle plants that he finds.

Nicely arranged is Leo's place,
like an untouched forest space.
Feeling so at home is a treat.
All that's missing is a bite to eat.

The task of buying fruit remains.
Globi spares no expense or pains.
What matters most is that it's nice,
though quality comes at a price.

His shopping bag, full of good food,
puts him in an excellent mood.
He hurries back, quite elated,
to the jungle he has created.

Leo Stays in Quarantine

Daydreaming while running mad,
creates danger to be had.
Like when Globi forgets to hop
over the janitor's misplaced mop.

Whoops! He falls, the fruit is flying,
then flat on the floor he's lying.
"Ow! My foot!" is Globi's cry.
Next the cleaner's feet will fly!

When there's fear of a broken bone,
an x-ray is taken to quiet the moan.
Dr. Klaus tells Globi, "Hold still,
and all will be fine. Yes it will!"

Globi's foot, though swollen, is whole,
no bone broken from ankle to sole.
The doctor says, "It's sprained, but sound."
Globi now looks out for brooms, all around.

With brooms as crutches he will go,
and be happy with things, just so,
for Leo's place is just a few yards,
and feeding time is on the cards.

The doctor and the cleaner are pleased
at the chance that Globi has seized.
"Brooms as crutches? That's quite clever.
What an ingenious endeavour!"

At the Airport Doctor

At check-in nervous travellers fear
that if all is not done with care,
the conveyor belt will sound an alarm.
A worried girl's doll falls from her arm.

"Oh no, my doll is going away!"
cries the little girl. Globi steps up to say,
"No problem." Straight in he dives,
because he leaps, his efforts thrive.

The baggage swirling all about
is imposing, there is no doubt.
Along the black belt Globi sprawls,
quickly towards the doll he crawls.

Globi grabs the doll at full speed,
but he forgets he should take heed,
and all at once it is too late,
he passes through the monitor's gate.

Then everything's x-rayed and seen.
An alarm flashes on the screen.
The inspector is quite unnerved
when a skeleton is observed.

The amazed woman is seeing
a remarkable blue being,
who from the conveyor belt springs,
and with him a little doll flings.

Alarm at the Baggage-Check

A trip with children can be a treat,
but parents crave quiet when they eat.
Globi shows these parents the way
to the nursery, where children play.

Here children feel that they are blessed,
and their parents feel it no less.
Louder, the clamouring voices grow,
but only Globi sees it's so.

The woman says she cannot stay,
for a short time, she must be away.
"Globi," she says, "please be a dear,
and make sure all stays peaceful here."

The havoc explodes like a bomb.
Should Globi simply remain calm?
Or must from him at once be heard
a very clear, definite word?

Neither, yet. The children need first
a world in which to be immersed.
Globi brings this with fantasy,
spirit and pleasant harmony.

He puts on a play with just his socks,
and soon the children's sights are locked.
There is great cheer, nothing is marred.
Minding children seems not so hard.

In the Nursery

Many cases, boxes and crates
are rushed to the jet as it waits.
The conveyor belt is put in place,
which brings a smile to Globi's face.

"Before we load, if I have fun,
it can't do harm to anyone."
He climbs up on the belt and sits
on a box, amidst bags, he fits.

Soon he arrives up at the top.
He moves with care, nothing will drop.
But now the boxes block the floor.
Globi piles them up, more and more.

He moves the cartons all around.
His pride in his work is profound.
"This space is now splendidly neat!"
He smiles at his impressive feat.

With cartons piled up to a human's height –
alas, the job is not done right,
the stacks obstruct Globi's way back.
Suddenly, everything looks black.

Is he seen by one of the staff?
Yes, he can even hear a laugh.
"Can it be? How's this come about?"
"Don't worry, I will get you out."

Loading Must Be Learned

Unloading luggage sometimes brings
slight damage to certain things.
Quite enchanted, the big snake sees,
her cover has slipped off by degrees.

From out of her large, darkened crate
towards the runway she slithers straight.
Globi calls out, but pointlessly,
as such snakes are quite deaf, you see.

Moving a boa is very hard,
one must really be on guard.
Two hundred and twenty pounds it weighs,
they strain, but on the ground it stays.

Now the snake has fallen asleep,
so Globi needn't think very deep.
He's off to the storehouse nearby,
it soon becomes very clear why.

Dollies, which are used to carry
loads out of the ordinary,
will achieve the desired outcome
with this great beast so cumbersome.

This method was luckily found.
The dollies are now quickly bound
to the belly of the huge snake.
Now moving him is a piece of cake.

The Giant Snake

Cartons full of orchid plants,
cacti and many succulents[1]
arrive in the cargo of a jumbo jet.
Globi must see if they carry a threat.

He quickly loads all the cases
filled with plants from different places
on the handy forklift machine.
It's all part of the routine.

He drives quickly, as it's crucial,
to the plant customs official.
Boxes are opened and laid bare,
customs papers studied with care.

She's looking for tiny creatures,
these are most unwanted features
in plants arriving from abroad.
They destroy plants, this tiny horde.

Globi would like to see the pest
which, though it likes orchids best,
does not other favourites lack.
Even cucumbers he'll attack!

This nasty, evil plant eater
measures just a millimetre.
Each plant thus needs close inspection
to provide us all with protection.

1 juice-filled plants that grow in very dry regions

Plant Inspection

Today Globi wants to explore
the great airport from floor to floor.
Leo wants to join him, that's made clear.
"Help!" screams Margaret in fear.

"She is locked in, my little girl!"
Margaret cries, her mind in a whirl.
"My child is crying in the WC.
Help me quickly. Please come see!"

Margaret's self-control is slight,
"Now I will surely miss my flight!"
Leo hangs onto Globi tight.
As they rush off as fast as they might.

For a good locksmith to be sought
and to release the girl who is caught
would take at least an hour or two.
But Leo is here to see it through!

Small rescuers can save much time
if doors they can easily climb.
Inside, Leo holds the handle fast
and turns till it gives way at last.

All could not have gone more correctly.
"My little girl returned directly!
Many thanks to the clever pair.
Leo, your help's beyond compare!"

Locked In

This lady can't find her suitcase,
it's disappeared without a trace.
Off to the lost baggage office
Globi intends to find what's missed.

"Suitcases we have, don't worry,
a huge number, but do not hurry,"
laughs the man. "And please look with care.
Perhaps you will find it in there."

"If only," sighs Globi, "that were so."
Because the woman does not know,
she is not sure – at quite a cost! –
which of those suitcases she has lost.

"It can't be found? That I doubt.
Let's have your little dog sniff it out!
A dog's nose is by far the best,"
Globi is happy to suggest.

Sniffing through the big storage space,
the small dog moves at quite a pace.
Soon amidst the shelves one can hear
a dog's bark, loud, proud and clear.

The barking is just to indicate
the suitcase is found – not too late.
"Well done," the woman says amazed.
Globi smiles; it's nice to be praised.

The Nose Knows

In the lift, on the upward ride
everyone's patience is tried,
because, before the second floor,
the lift stops, and will go no more.

Globi, feeling trapped suddenly,
at once presses decisively
the button to sound the alarm,
used for moments of possible harm.

The building's control central
registers the alarm signal.
It can automatically tell
which lift transmitted it as well.

Since calls come in at a great rate,
some calls, of course, have to wait.
Globi's anger has taken its toll,
so he messes with the control.

After all this button-bashing,
the panel gets a full thrashing.
With all his strength he gives a kick –
a click, it whirrs! "That did the trick!"

There's something odd and curious
in store for 'Globi the Furious.'
It seems someone was there to help,
the electrician, Mr Phelp.

A Stubborn Lift

Globi sits in the flight simulator
and flies calmly to the Equator.
This outing of aerial bliss
is aviation training for Swiss.[1]

Shapely clouds roll and flow,
lightning flashes, a storm brews below.
He hears the thunder loudly sound,
it's no longer safe to fly around.

Fully caught is the airplane,
colour from Globi's face drains.
In the simulator he begins to sweat,
where he is, he did forget.

Now flames shoot from the fuselage!
Gathering up his deepest courage,
Globi tries, once more in the storm,
to see what controls still perform.

Globi soon feels in his own seat
something like the inferno's heat.
Then the emergency system fails.
"Help! I want to get out!" he wails.

Engine damage, thunder, lightning,
rumbles, heat and smoke so frightening.
The simulation was so strikingly real.
For Globi, this has no appeal.

1 Swiss Aviation Training is an organisation belonging to Swiss for
  professional pilots, cabin personnel and airplane mechanics

Only the Fear Was Real

To move quickly underground,
passengers need not wait around.
So begins many a long flight,
Skymetro[1] is a traveller's delight.

Suddenly there's desperation,
what was once a huge, bright station
has now become pitch black as night.
Is this some joker's act of spite?

Globi, who's also in the throng,
doesn't need to think for long.
He decides that it's his mission
to call for a skilled electrician.

Then to a shop he goes in haste
and returns with a heavy case.
Now happily he walks about,
He's brought torches to hand out.

And thanks to many a new light,
other faces, too, now look bright.
People hurry through the station
securely to their destination.

The electrician changes fast
the fuses. The crisis has passed,
Globi's help has been essential,
light will shine at full potential.

---

1 Skymetro is an underground, compressed air train held up by steel cables,
which connects the Airside Center with Dock E.

Electrical Failure in the Station

Taking this small train to Terminal E
is just as pleasant as can be,
for the Skymetro is more, we think,
than just a simple railway link.

To ride it isn't just to hover,
it also gives time to discover
many treasures of Switzerland
seen on tunnel walls where you stand.

Mooing and a yodelling refrain
echo loudly throughout the train.
The passengers express surprise,
there's more here than meets the eye.

Instead of scenes usually here,
much stranger pictures appear.
A figure sitting on a cow?
Globi! That's really something, now!

The one riding here, long before,
made the changes seen – and more.
Globi's perfectly played his joke.
Is he a new star among the folk?

All those riding aboard agree
that Globi is a treat to see
riding on a cow today.
People laugh, as they go their way.

Surprise in the Skymetro

Lots of travellers hope to be spared
the question, "Are your goods declared?"
But the law makes no exception,
all must submit to an inspection.

Globi is also asked today
to have his bag checked along the way.
From the wheeled suitcase just before,
comes a loud "beep" one can't ignore.

Is there perhaps a threat inside?
Take no risks — quickly run and hide.
It's bad enough to fear attack,
especially when you hear a "Quack."

And then the thing begins to go
on two feet, if at first still slow,
it hurries on at a great stride.
Bewildered, Globi runs beside.

Through the hall, the bulging suitcase
staggers like a dizzy man in a race.
Those who see it reeling about
wonder how this will all turn out.

Globi grabs the suitcase at last,
and pulls the cover off it fast.
An ostrich stares at him, now mum.
Globi smiles. What an odd outcome!

The Eerie Suitcase

A necessary airport stop
is a visit to the gift shop.
Globi enters and chooses here
a clock as a nice souvenir.

To a workshop he goes that day
to saw, file and hammer away,
until it seems a new tick-tock
emerges from the store-bought clock.

The present is packed to be sent,
by quick hands, with little time spent.
At the post office he asks, "Say,
how can this arrive next day?"

The present has arrived without doubt.
"How could Globi have figured out
that I like Swiss cuckoo clocks so?"
Grandma Hedwig would like to know.

As viewers all anticipate,
right at the hour, and not too late,
there's a click which opens the spring,
and a merry bird is heard to sing.

The door opens and "Cuckoo," is heard,
but the sound comes from a strange bird.
Grandma is delighted to see
it's Globi calling happily.

A Present for Grandma

For each traveller in an airplane seat,
Gate Gourmet[1] provides food to eat,
but the Chef can't make up his mind,
which dessert would be the best kind.

Globi thinks, for this creation,
fruit is ripe for experimentation.
By the banana he is inspired,
it's precisely what's required.

A half banana, cut length-wise,
Globi thinks is just the right size.
On a plate with lots of whipped cream,
it will look just like a dream.

Along the whipped cream he places,
by the sides in even spaces,
fresh pineapple in four sections.
Globi loves kitchen confections.

For the next step he'll be using
strawberries that he has been choosing.
Globi adorns these in tandem
with pastry icing. Just random?

No! In the head of this brisk youth
the dessert was all planned, in truth.
Then he went and carried it through.
Amazing, what Globi can do!

1 A gourmet is a person who appreciates fine food.

An Airplane to Bite Into

Lotte, alone, with no other,
is off to visit her godmother
in Paris. But here is her plight,
she has no escort for the flight!

"Globi, do you also work here?
Could you accompany my dear?"
the mother asks with a hopeful sigh.
Globi listens, and then asks, "Why?"

"Alone, my little girl can't fly
to Orly near Paris, and I
can't go with her," she explains now.
 "I'll do it!" is Globi's vow.

A new UM's[1] waiting in Datong[2]
for an escort to come along.
"Please show boarding card and passport."
"Sorry," Globi says, coming up short.

"One may, in cases of this sort,
request an emergency passport,"
explains the uniformed man.
Globi is delighted that he can.

But then everything moves quite fast,
after a few minutes have passed,
a perfect passport for Globi.
A new fashion trend? It just might be!

1 "UM" is the abbreviation for Unaccompanied Minor.
2 a city in China

Flight Accompaniment

Rather nervous, Globi wonders,
do security ever make blunders?
Or can one absolutely rely
on being protected when you fly?

Before going through the big gate,
the next man doesn't hesitate
to give up his jacket and hat,
shampoo, liquid soap, and all that.

Then from Marianne, straight away,
Globi receives a plastic tray,
on which all his metal objects go.
Globi arranges them just so.

Up to the gate he quickly moves,
but there are problems, as it proves.
The metal detector beeps very loud.
Globi is embarrassed in the crowd.

"The detector will beep away
until trousers, not just beret,
on the conveyor belt also lie,"
Marianna explains with a sigh.

Globi is completely depressed,
as now he finds he's barely dressed.
He marches outraged through the gate.
Watchers smile wisely at his fate.

Globi's Security Check

The sky is completely blue and fair,
there's no turbulence in the air.
So on this flight Captain Heinz Rot
names Globi as his 'co-pilot.'

"Just hold the controls and glide."
No, that's not enough Globi decides.
He presses buttons when they blink.
What's wrong with him? What does he think?

Heinz Rot grabs the controls in fear.
"This is outrageous! Do you hear?
You've played around without a care!"
Globi deserves Rot's angry stare.

The airplane is badly shaken,
jolted in the turns it's taken.
That's damage enough for one day.
Captain Rot takes the controls away.

"You have created quite a mess."
Globi blinks sadly in distress.
"Go back to the cabin and see
what the passengers' needs might be."

His punishment is not neglected.
This is not what he expected.
Shamefaced, he walks down the aisle
collecting sick bags all the while.

From Co-Pilot to Steward

"Look, winding in and out again,
you see that river? That's the Seine.
And the Eiffel Tower is over there.
Paris is wonderful, I do declare!"

In the airport's huge arrival hall,
Lotte sees through the windows all
who are waiting there. She runs to greet
her French godmother. What a treat!

The luggage belt is long awake,
and circles like a giant snake.
Suddenly Globi is afraid.
Has the child's suitcase been mislaid?

Amongst the cases that abound,
moving endlessly round and round,
no surprise that the case slips by,
without it catching Globi's eye.

Now it threatens to disappear
through the luggage hatch, free and clear.
Globi is determined to give it chase,
and just manages to grab Lotte's case.

He proudly brings his rescued prize
to Lotte who greets him with wide eyes.
"Bonjour![2] Hello!" he calls with glee.
She happily responds, "Merci,[3] Globi".

1 French: meeting
2 French: Hello
3 French: Thank you

Rendezvous[1] at Paris-Orly

"Let's visit the control tower.
You can see in just one hour
what the Skyguides[1] must do all day,"
the controller offers. "Okay?"

A controller shows on the screen
multitudes of points to be seen.
The points all serve to indicate
what's flying where, and at what rate.

"You understand it all, I see.
Will you please take over for me
while I go get something to eat?"
Globi's flattered, and takes his seat.

It's strange. The screen signals increase
all at once, and do not cease.
There's so much traffic in the air,
controllers must take extra care.

Globi sweats from every pore:
a fully crammed air corridor.
And as if that were not enough,
other signals make the job tough.

The controllers laugh in full view:
"We tried to have a go at you."
Then they explain, still elated,
"Everything was simulated."

1 name of the Swiss air traffic controllers

In the Tower

Short time between flights is significant,
so the cleaning crew must be efficient.
Everyone must be quite ready
so the job's done sure and steady.

The cleaners have all decided
how the work will be divided.
Globi will first hoover the floor,
that's one task, but there are more.

After the vacuuming is done,
he finds materials that one
needs most to clean the kitchen well.
Scrubbing's tiring, as you can tell.

Then the toilet must be made clean,
so it's a place fit to be seen.
Spick and span and disinfected.[1]
All goes well, nothing's neglected.

When cleaning is done, without delay,
objects must be taken away.
Some are trash, but amidst all this,
are many things someone would miss.

Books, bears, shoes from different places,
umbrellas, mobile phone cases,
hats, cameras lying around,
they all go to the Lost-and-Found.

1 made free of germs

Finders Keepers?

Pushing, that's Globi's job today,
a large jet to the taxiway.
He climbs in the vehicle to see
just how difficult this can be.

Soon he hears the starting call, "Go!"
Just how the controls function, though,
Globi is not too sure about.
He figures he'll just try them out.

He drives, but almost into a wall.
The pilot is not pleased at all.
He leans out the cockpit to shout.
Globi's confused and looks about.

Being in charge of controls
is a task for patient souls.
He turns, and this pulls the jet's nose,
copying him, to the side it goes.

The danger is thus averted,
but Globi must be alerted
to cease this mad turning around.
"Stop right now!" is the angry sound.

Instead of stopping as he should,
Globi ran as fast as he could!
He leaves the tug far behind,
men chase him, but he pays no mind.

The Airplane Carousel

Something's been beeping for an hour
on Heinz's screen in the tower.
But only now has he seen
the alarm flashing on the screen.

Heinz asks an old hand named Frank.
Frank's answer seems part of a prank,
"Well, it must be a UFO[1],
only they would signal like so."

Fritz too begins to fool around.
"If you hear such a signal sound,
it's old St Nicholas gone out
with his sleigh to ride about."

They're mocking him, Heinz surmises.
He'll see if Globi realises
what's moving eastward in the sky.
Binoculars might help him try.

After brief investigation,
he gives his interpretation.
Globi says, "Neither of them is right.
What's flying is . . . no, not a kite."

"Tell us," the other two demand,
suspense is something they can't stand.
"A stork sending information
about their annual migration."

1 unidentified flying object

The Phantom UFO

Runways must be cleaned frequently,
for, otherwise, subsequently
if the runway is not completely clear,
a plane might get a flat tyre here.

Globi collects in a hurry
sharp objects that can cause worry.
Although the runway's now secure,
there are other dangers, to be sure!

Driver Peter points to the sky
as a great mass of birds fly by.
Starlings tend to fly in a swarm,
especially when it's warm.

In autumn one has to watch out
when swarms of starlings are about.
For the turbines, both large and small,
are damaged in no time at all.

"With swarms of starlings," says Globi,
"loud noises will always make them flee."
"Pot lids?" Peter laughs, quite amused.
Globi demonstrates how they're used.

But Peter thinks it's not enough,
a flare gun will call their bluff.
Soon he chases the birds away
with a bang; all choose not to stay.

On the Runway Check

Sometimes the animals seen here
can be unusual, that is clear.
Ornithologist[1] Lorenz shows
the visitors how much he knows.

First a view of a falcon's flight,
next the group views with great delight
a lapwing in the open field.
The visitors walk on with their eyes peeled.

"In that young willow over there
lurks a furry creature, I declare!
Could it have escaped from the zoo?"
a boy asks, surprised by his view.

"It's a cat from the neighbourhood,
who'd catch a sparrow if he could,"
declares Lorenz with spirits high.
Then he looks, and lets out a sigh.

Through binoculars, unlike before,
he can see it's an omnivore.[2]
He now states, "No more to discuss.
It's a leontopithecus!"[3]

To Lorenz, something is not clear.
"Where is he from? Was he brought here?"
Perhaps he will soon realise
this is Globi's kind of surprise.

1 someone who studies birds and bird behaviour
2 animal that eats both vegetable and animal matter
3 name of the animal family to which the lion monkey belongs

Surprise in the Conservation Area

Birds nearby make pilots worry,
problems occur in a hurry.
Their danger cannot be forgot,
if the big birds fly in that spot.

Next to the runways, on the land,
there are many animals to hand.
Near Kloten many mice stay,
and buzzards carry some away.

Swiss farmers say, "Few mice, few birds."
In that old saying, these are the words.
Therefore each year with great effort,
the rodents are carefully caught.

Globi doesn't think long before
he recalls the rat catcher of yore –
named the Pied Piper of Hamelin.[1]
"That will solve the fix they're in!"

With the sounds of the flute he plays,
Globi lures mice from their hideaways.
The herd of mice grows and grows
inconceivably as he goes.

He lures, with the notes of his flute,
hundreds of mice along a route
away from where the buzzards wait.
Planes will be safer now – that's great!

1 The Pied Piper of Hamelin" – a German legend

The Pied Piper of the Airport

Midnight has now already passed
when two quiet carts roll up fast.
Cleaning items in them abound.
Ann leads novice Globi around.

First Globi must sweep with the broom,
then empty baskets in the room
full of piled-up rubbish and such.
Globi wipes up all the muck.

He cleans intensely and can't stop,
his only companion is his mop.
Soon the Bye-Bye-Bar is clean,
ready again to prepare cuisine.

Globi cleans with two hands,
saving time is part of his plan.
Though everything goes twice as quick,
he's still quite professional and slick.

The broad, smooth surface of the floor
comforts and relaxes him even more.
While sitting on the sweeper there
he can clean well, without a care.

At the departures board, at last,
working so hard, he tires fast.
Asleep now, from cleaning he's freed.
This we can call "finished" indeed.

Spick and Span and Finished

Early in the morn without thought,
Globi, in deep sleep, is brought
on a stretcher to the dayroom,
for more sleep one can presume.

Globi, held in Morpheus'[1] arms,
fast asleep he fears no harm.
He's unaware that he's been taken,
lying on the bed, he'll not awaken.

Not long does he wallow in dreams
of perfectly cleaned rooms, it seems.
Suddenly he's assailed by sound
of volume and strangeness profound.

The source of disruption is vague.
What are these noises that plague
and drag him from his dream?
The volume is really quite extreme!

Into the passage creeps Globi.
He opens the door tentatively,
inch by inch, and before him sees
people celebrating as they please!

Cancelled was their connecting flight,
so they have made light of their plight
with their hometown celebration,
an Indian meditation.

1 Greek god of dreams

A Celebration in the Dayrooms

Good food, two times every day,
helps in-between time pass away.
Globi brings for Leo's meal
a bowl of fruit, which is ideal.

"Leo, come here and get your food,"
Globi says in a helpful mood.
But the dog, seeing the feeding,
barks, halting the proceeding.

Leo is scared out of his wits,
he's not tempted by the tasty bits.
In panic, Leo flees from there.
Globi follows that mop of hair!

Though Globi can run quite quick,
Leo too knows many a trick.
He escapes through the open door,
and upsets Globi more and more.

Through the waiting room Leo tears,
people shriek as they stare.
Globi hisses, sounding severe,
"Just wait, I'm sure to catch you here!"

Leo spots greenery up high,
and now the lion monkey flies!
Up the wall covered in plants,
he escapes Globi's advance.

Leo in Panic

Will Globi manage to succeed
at catching up to Leo's lead?
No, the monkey has won this time,
he's perched calmly after his climb.

Leo sticks out his tongue at Globi
and laughs, as cheeky as can be.
Leo just loves to play the clown,
the game is one-nil, Globi's down.

I'm going up, decides Globi,
and I will catch that monkey!
To Globi Gardener Klaus lends
a platform hoist, to make amends.

What's designed to clean the leaves here
might work as monkey-catching gear.
Lifted by magic hands unseen,
Globi rides up the wall of green.

Ten full meters above the ground,
Globi must choose a method sound.
He will trap Leo with his hat,
he knows he is quite good at that.

Policemen patrol the grounds,
but Globi's cunning knows no bounds.
With Leo under his beret,
nothing will get in his way.

A Catch with a Hat

On the truck that Horst has brought here,
a tank is missing – that seems clear.
Globi sees the truck has a hose,
through which much liquid flows.

Globi is surprised to hear
the fuel is stored in tanks quite near.
They're situated underground,
the truck will bring the hose around.

Hardly is the hose connected
when Globi has smoke detected.
In woods nearby it swirls about,
"Come on, Horst, let's go put it out!"

They pull up to the local brook,
the hose is taken off its hook
and then brought to the water fast.
The hose supports are set down last.

From the truck's highest position
he sprays water with precision
into the nearby clump of trees.
But his satisfaction quickly flees.

"You've ruined our wonderful campfire!"
the wet scouts all shout, full of ire.
Some fires must be kept lit,
to serve purpose in a pit.

False Alarm

Today the airport is quite a scene,
from London has come the Queen.
All are excited, but far too loud,
policemen try to manage the crowd.

Confusion prevails in the mass
few are able to easily pass.
A sly hat thief finds this just right
for the next theft he has in sight.

But what this man now plans to do
is not concealed from Globi's view.
Alarmed by the pole that appears,
Globi will prevent what he fears.

Suddenly, with menacing snaps,
the man opens the picker's flaps.
With cunning and intention mean
they snap at the hat of the Queen.

Globi knocks the pole down flat,
he's never scared to act like that.
The royal Queen, who is so amused,
praises the skill that Globi used.

As an escort, the Queen will need
one who has such courage indeed.
Globi is, by royal command,
to accompany her throughout the land.

The Queen and the Hat Thief

A balloon has gone badly astray,
caution is needed right away.
The tower sends out the alarm
hoping to prevent any harm.

Because the wind that's blowing here
blows stronger and won't disappear,
the skies turn menacingly gray.
How can Globi save the day?

He decides he knows what to do,
race with blue light and siren through
from the field station just nearby
towards the balloon in the sky.

Stealthily, the balloon moves right,
into the landing airplane's flight.
A rope is thrown down at this sight,
because time remaining is so tight.

Within ten seconds, and not more,
the rope is made quite secure.
Globi pulls, as if in a race,
the balloon to a safer place.

Now they've landed! Without delay,
Globi is thanked for saving the day
by the Captain, whose pleasure shows,
"Globi, you're really on your toes!"

A Balloon Gone Astray

To the deck for observation
children run with animation.
Even the parents love the show
of airplanes flying to and fro.

They land, load, take off and fly.
Binoculars give every eye
much to observe and learn about.
Lynn is the first to try them out.

Globi, after a little while,
then helps Melinda, Fritz and Kyle.
But Oscar's weight is so much
he nearly loses his touch.

Globi is unaccustomed to stay
and lift up children every day.
In his arms he feels much pain,
he never wants to lift again.

How to continue this way
without causing a delay?
Before he starts to panic
he'll visit the mechanic.

Globi now finds it easy as pie
to raise the small children up high
using the lifting jack as a lever.
Globi can be truly clever.

On the Observation Deck

The landing of the jet is marred
by turbulence, which makes it hard.
The wind pushes up the plane's tail,
passengers fear the plane might fail!

The nose wheel jolts on the runway,
makes it smoke. This is not okay.
Now engine oil starts to drip,
which could ignite the flight strip.

Globi saw the smoke when it landed
and knows action is now demanded.
He's at the engine, unafraid,
"It's a job for the Fire Brigade!"

Our team rushes at breakneck pace
like a rocket through outer space,
with siren screams not abating
to the runway, where the jet is waiting.

A fire engine soon arrives,
well prepared to save lives.
With the hose Globi won't tire,
and he's soon busy with the fire.

There isn't any time to wait,
out of the pipe the spray shoots straight.
Globi puts the fire right out,
from the cockpit comes a happy shout.

The Fire Brigade in Action

Now in the hangar with haste
the nose wheel[1] is to be replaced.
The small tug used for such runs
can pull planes of two hundred tons!

Next mechanics demonstrate
how they change wheels at a quick rate.
Now a mechanic turns to say,
"Please bring a new wheel right away."

Globi tries to carry the wheel,
but the weight is an ordeal.
He realises, before too long,
it'd be better if he were strong.

Globi's not strong, but he has a brain.
He can be clever with no strain.
Globi looks carefully around
and soon some helium[2] is found.

What makes balloons hang in the air
will surely serve this weight to bear!
So Globi quickly fills the tyre
with the gas the task requires.

The mechanics gasp at the sight,
here comes someone, puny and slight,
with a huge tyre ready at hand.
Look what brains can do on command!

1 Even when there are two wheels, it is still called the nose wheel.
2 Non-flammable gas, seven times lighter than air. Used to fill balloons.

Easy Wheel Change

Agile Globi quickly tries out
hand signals he learned about.
The signs worldwide are all the same,
motions too numerous to name.

This signal means *more to the right;*
but if done in mirror's sight,
to the left, the reflection states.
This joke Globi appreciates.

In order to signal in the night,
one needs rods that give off light.
But in daytime no one's confused
if red signal discs are also used.

Globi practises every sign
that is displayed in the chart's design.
Then he begins to add a few.
He's so proud of what he can do.

Globi starts his frenzied prancing,
mixing signals while dancing.
Globi frolics this way and that,
he's a break-dancing acrobat.

At last Globi sees, in a daze,
the result of his eager ways,
on the holding field near the gate.
Upset, he signals to them, *wait.*

Globi Forgets Himself

If students are eager to learn
nothing else is a concern.
Putting out a fire is today
taught in a very detailed way.

To listen and look is demanding,
but then must come understanding,
so they end this education
with practical application.

Amongst the little study class
only Globi notices, alas,
on the hilltop, smoke has come,
this is no holiday custom!

Without considering until late,
the pros and cons to debate,
Globi rushes across the land,
a fire extinguisher in hand.

There he is surrounded by smoke
like never in his life – no joke! –
He sprays the CO_2 [1] about,
until the fire's completely out.

But this, his life's crowning glory,
is actually a worthless story.
Everything was simulated.
Globi's pride is much deflated.

1 Formula for the gas carbon dioxide, which, like powder and foam, is used in
hand-held fire extinguishers.

Serious Fire Practice

Today a small revelation
in front of the weather station.
Many tools are shown,
only three of which are known.

The particular need is expressed
for certain things to be assessed,
like clouds and visibility.
Hey! What flies with such agility?

Look, those are cranes southward flying!
The cold winter they are trying
to escape by going south in flight.
Migrations are a lovely sight.

Since the cranes sense a storm,
Globi runs off to inform
the airport's old weatherman
that snow will cover the land.

But the man laughingly queries,
"Have you support for these theories?"
Yet now he observes silently,
that the screen blinks violently.

"The weather will be bad today,"
to the public he's heard to say,
"and a heavy snowstorm is in sight."
Globi feels self-righteous delight.

Globi the Weatherman

Beep! Beep! Off the pager goes,
before the rooster has even crowed.
Yet again it raises Globi,
who rubs his eyes sleepily.

Globi must be off, it's quite clear why.
Flakes are swirling, the snow is piled high.
Everyone hurries to their plough,
then to the holding field somehow.

Globi's crew, as assembled before,
follows the tower's words as law.
They serve throughout the entire night
before the coming of morning light.

With his plough Globi takes the lead,
a practised snowplough man, indeed.
With deliberation and care,
he steers into the white snow's glare.

All other drivers then must see
they should line up behind Globi.
That's their responsibility.
Careful planning is the key.

In a 'V' they must drive, in fact,
and keep the formation intact.
They clear runways without delay,
until all snow is ploughed away.

Runway Clearance

Fixing the lighting is on the list
of things to do that Globi missed.
One runway light is defective,
the lights need a quick corrective.

This was done by the snowy gale
as told to Globi in detail.
He's assigned to fix it with Yves,
but their efforts bring no reprieve.

One cannot walk across slick ice
without slipping once or twice.
There simply is no time to wait,
the need for safety is too great.

The jet de-icer 'elephant'
now suddenly seems relevant.
It has just sprayed a large plane,
Globi needs it to work again.

Globi has not too long to wait
because the jet takes off straight
away leaving the de-icer free,
ready to be used by Globi.

Soon the ice is melting away,
Globi and Yves display
anticipation, for they see
they can repair the light shortly.

Practical De-Icer

A ski lift has an urgent plight,
there is damage that can't be put right.
A replacement part is needed now.
"Airport, do you have one around?"

The pilot gives the okay,
Globi will join him on the way.
Now the helicopter can start
transporting the replacement part.

This trip has really been a must,
the job is done without a fuss.
Can the helicopter then wait?
Or must it return home straight?

The pilot makes his return run,
but Globi stays to have some fun.
With the help of the replaced part,
he can enjoy the snow at last.

On the old part Globi springs,
he curves and loops, as if with wings,
riding along his downhill way –
the purest winter sport ballet.

"Hey!" someone is heard to say.
"That boy took the piece away
to use for his snowboarding fun.
This sort of thing should not be done."

Delivery by Helicopter

Globi has come to visit Leo,
who leaps upon him with brio.
Globi can't help but smile,
"Quiet down Leo, for a while".

Then off to the doctor's they start,
who will check Leo's heart.
The veterinarian's glad
that Leo does not move a tad.

"The quarantine has now ended,"
states Hotz. "Leo you are splendid.
You've passed the health tests perfectly.
Leo, you're as healthy as can be!"

Globi paints a future scene,
"Leo, wait till you have seen
the magnificent Zurich Zoo.
There are other lion monkeys too."

Leo no longer feels withdrawn,
his homesickness is all gone.
He leaps around in merriment,
unable to contain excitement.

"Leo, time to be on our way,
but first stop is the Director to say,
'Goodbye,'" Globi suggests.
"Then we'll complete our quest!"

Leo May Enter the Zoo

They've been expected for a while.
They're greeted in a pleasant style,
"I envy you – indeed I do.
The Director is waiting just for you."

For Globi he has special praise,
"On each of these several days,
there is much about you I've heard.
Everyone has said a good word.

"Globi, you were oft applauded,
as a 'professional' commended.
So it was easy to decide,
you will be our Honorary Guide."

Globi's pleased by his cap so chic.
It's useful and indeed unique,
For his work so highly rated
Globi is now celebrated.

"Globi is hurrying to the Zoo,
and with him Leo's coming too!"
Now seven steps lead to the Zoo,
praise is awaiting them there, too.

"That's great, Globi," observes Hector,
the world-famous Zoo Director.
Leo now settles down very fast
in the comfort of friends at last.

Bye-Bye Airport

Dear Friends of Globi,

Like Globi, you have now become acquainted with the airport. No doubt you would also like to learn how the airport actually began and how it has changed over the years.

The construction of Zurich Airport began in 1946. A great deal of manual labour was required, as the machines that we use today did not exist yet. Two years later, the first airplanes took off from and landed on the new runways. The airport was then further developed and completed while it was in operation. It was not until five years later, in 1953, that the great opening celebration took place. People from all over the world were invited to celebrate the opening of the new airport and to marvel at the air show.

More and more airlines began to arrive in Zurich during the following years, so the airport had to be expanded. The airplanes were also becoming larger. In 1970 the first jumbo jet landed at the airport. This was, until recently, the largest airplane in the world. In order for the air travellers to travel conveniently to the airport itself, the underground airport train station was built in 1980. The Queen of England actually took part in the opening ceremonies.

Zurich Airport celebrated its 50th birthday in 1998. Part of the ceremony was the visit of the Concorde from France. At that time it was the fastest, and loudest, passenger airplane in the world. That year, 21 million passengers passed through Zurich Airport. This was three times as many air travellers as 18 years earlier. Three years later, the airport was in a panic over a great crisis. The famous airline Swissair no longer had enough money and had to stop flying. This was referred to as a "grounding." Many passengers were stuck in Zurich Airport and could no longer find departing flights.

Between 2000 and 2004, the airport was largely renovated. The Airside Centre, the building with many windows, was also built during this period. Today, Zurich Airport is the best airport in Europe. It has developed into a proper city, visited daily by 70,000 people on average.

Occupations at Zurich Airport

Occupations at Zurich Airport

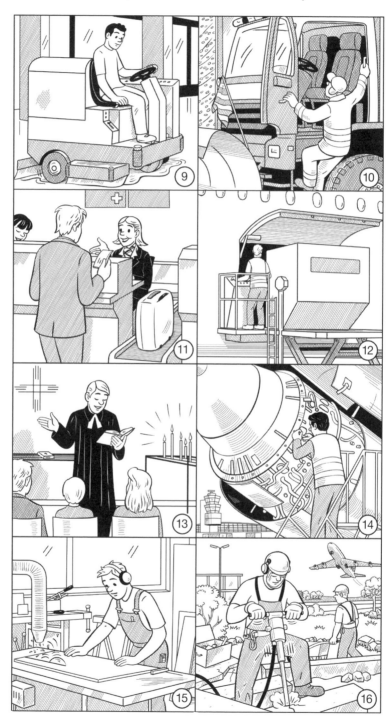

1. Pilot
   The pilot's responsibilities include commanding the airplane in a safe and economical manner, flight preparation, carefully following regulations and close cooperation with ground personnel and air traffic controllers.

2. Flight Attendant / Cabin Crew Member
   This profession includes varied and important responsibilities: caring for the passengers, the implementation of security measures and in-flight service.

3. Professional Fire fighter
   Professional fire fighters work at all hours of the day and night to fight fires, rescue people, animals and valuables, and also take part mountain rescue and recovery following accidents and thunderstorms.

4. Airport Police
   The airport police carefully check everyone who wishes to enter Switzerland. They deny entry to people who want to do anything illegal. They ensure that no one damages the aircraft or steals suitcases. They help people who cannot find their way around the airport or who have had anything stolen.

5. Gardener
   Airport gardeners are specialists in decorative plants. They care for and sell flowers, bushes and trees in their own gardens. They arrange the plants and create and care for green spaces.

6. Tour Guide and Bus Driver
   The tour guide leads tour groups through the airport. There are various guided tours through which one can become well acquainted with the airport and learn how it operates.

   The bus driver drives passengers to their flights and picks up arriving passengers at their airplanes to drive them to the arrival hall.

   The bus drivers and the tour guides also offer sightseeing tours along the airport ramp where they show tour groups the airport's operations.

7. Air Traffic Controller
   Air traffic controllers ensure that aircrafts always maintain sufficient distance from each other and that air traffic moves safely. They give pilots permission to take-off and land, remain in contact with them throughout their flights, and help them to maintain their flight patterns in the air.

8. Sales Employee /
   Service Centre Staff Member
   In the Service Centre you meet people from a variety of nations and cultures every day. Here all manner of questions are answered and information is given out. The employees give advice and help. They must, therefore, have a good mastery of foreign languages and computer skills. They also sell concert tickets and advertising merchandise.

9. Cleaning Staff
   The cleaning staff use a variety of cleaning tools and methods to keep a wide variety of surfaces meticulous. They work during the early morning, in the evening or even during the night. It is very important that the airport be kept clean, so that passengers feel comfortable there.

10. Winter Road Clearance Driver
    The Winter Service organisation is responsible for organising of employees in winter. In the vast airport grounds, eight vehicles always drive together to keep the runways and taxi lanes free of snow, so that aircrafts can take off, land and taxi in safety.

11. Air Travellers Handling Agent
    The air travellers handling agents accept luggage at the check-in counter, check documentation, and give information about departure times and gates. At the gate, they coordinate boarding and answer questions. They also look after passengers in wheelchairs and children who are travelling alone. Travellers who must wait to continue their travels, or even spend the night in a hotel, are also attended to by the agents.

12. Operations Handling Agent

The operations handling agent transports luggage from the luggage storage area to the correct aircraft. The luggage is transported on small, connected tractors and loaded into the belly of the aircraft. Large airplanes are loaded with containers. Every day the operations handling agent lifts approximately 1000 pieces by hand. It is very difficult work, which must be performed outdoors in all kinds of weather.

13. Priest / Minister

In the airport chapel people can find a peaceful place. Here they can enjoy the quiet or participate in a religious service conducted by the airport minister. Sometimes passengers request a blessing for their journey. The minister is also there for conversations. Anyone can discuss their problems with him. Travellers, employees and visitors are happy that this possibility exists. The minister will not report to others anything that is said to him in confidence. He is bound professionally to maintain this secrecy.

14. Aircraft Mechanic

In the great halls, known as hangars, airplanes are checked regularly by the aircraft mechanics, and are repaired when necessary.

15. Joiners

The joiner at the airport is responsible for checking that doors and shutters function properly. He also repairs and replaces broken panes of glass. The joiner's skills as a craftsman are wide-ranging and widely applicable.

16. Rescue Engineer / Civil Defence

The Civil Defence at the airport helps the airport fire brigade, police and ambulance service when there is an emergency. To be able to do their work at any time, rescue engineers must regularly practise with large, heavy equipment (including excavators) and see to it that the machinery is functioning well and is always ready to be brought into action quickly.

We are grateful to **Monika Wirz,** Zurich Airport, of Corporate Communications, for her support in completing this book. She introduced us to all aspects of the airport and arranged contact with the various experts. She led the project with great commitment and good will.

Globi at the Airport
World Copyright © 2010
Globi Publishing, Imprint Orell Füssli Publishing AG, Zürich
www.globi.ch
1. Edition
ISBN 978-3-85703-375-9

Non-polluting printing and packaging

2010
Printer: Himmer AG, Augsburg